Room for More

MICHELLE KADARUSMAN

Illustrated by MAGGIE ZENG

pajamapress

First published in Canada and the United States in 2022

Text copyright © 2022 Michelle Kadarusman

Illustration copyright © 2022 Maggie Zeng

This edition copyright © 2022 Pajama Press Inc.

This is a first edition.

10 9 8 7 6 5 4 3 2 1

www.pajamapress.ca   info@pajamapress.ca

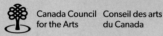   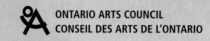   Canada

an Ontario government agency
un organisme du gouvernement de l'Ontario

The publisher gratefully acknowledges the support of the Canada Council for the Arts and the Ontario Arts Council for its publishing program. We acknowledge the financial support of the Government of Canada through the Canada Book Fund (CBF) for our publishing activities.

Library and Archives Canada Cataloguing in Publication
Title: Room for more / Michelle Kadarusman ; illustrated by Maggie Zeng.
Names: Kadarusman, Michelle, 1969- author. | Zeng, Maggie, illustrator.
Description: First edition.
Identifiers: Canadiana 20210395542 | ISBN 9781772782523 (hardcover)
Classification: LCC PS8621.A33 R66 2022 | DDC jC813/.6—dc23Publisher Cataloging-in-Publication Data (U.S.)

Publisher Cataloging-in-Publication Data (U.S.)
Names: Kadarusman, Michelle, 1969-, author. | Zeng, Maggie, illustrator.
Title: Room for More / Michelle Kadarusman ; illustrated by Maggie Zeng.
Description: Toronto, Ontario Canada : Pajama Press, 2022. | Summary: "In their burrow, wombats Dig and scratch are safe from an Australian bush fire. To Scratch's dismay, Dig invites two wallabies, a koala, and a tiger snake to join them. It's a tight squeeze, but even Scratch has to agree that welcoming their neighbors was a good idea when the other animals help the wombats through a flood. Back matter includes an author's note, a glossary of animals, and information about environmental disasters and Indigenous land stewardship"— Provided by publisher.
Identifiers: ISBN 978-1-77278-252-3 (hardcover)
Subjects: LCSH: Animals – Australia – Juvenile fiction. | Environmental disasters -- Juvenile fiction. | Wombats – Juvenile fiction. | Cooperation – Juvenile fiction. | BISAC: JUVENILE FICTION / Science & Nature / Disasters. | JUVENILE FICTION / Animals / General. | JUVENILE FICTION / Social Themes / Values & Virtues.
Classification: LCC PZ7. K333Ro |DDC [F] – dc23

Original art created digitally
Cover and book design—Lorena González Guillén

Printed in China by WKT Company

Pajama Press Inc.
11 Davies Ave., Suite 103, Toronto, Ontario, Canada M4M 2A9

Distributed in Canada by UTP Distribution
5201 Dufferin Street Toronto, Ontario Canada, M3H 5T8

Distributed in the U.S. by Ingram Publisher Services
1 Ingram Blvd. La Vergne, TN 37086, USA

To all who open their hearts,
homes, and borders to those in need
—M.K.

To my brother, Philip, my cousins,
Kathy and Vivian, and all my
wombat friends

—M.Z.

Two wombats, Dig and Scratch, peered out from the tunnel of their burrow. Their noses twitched.

"I smell smoke," said Dig.

"It's a bushfire!" cried Scratch.

"Don't worry," said Dig. "We'll be safe in here."

"It's a good thing we dug a nice, deep burrow,"
said Scratch. "Aren't we clever?"
"We are very lucky," agreed Dig.

Dig and Scratch hunkered down
in their wombat home, grateful
for the cool, damp chamber
that kept them safe from
the smoke and flames.

"I hear footsteps outside,"
said Scratch.

"Let's go and see,"
said Dig.

The wombats looked out from the tunnel and saw bush
animals scampering by, running to safety. Dig spied
a wallaby with a joey in her pouch. The mother
wallaby had stopped in her tracks.

"Come in here with us," Dig called
to them. "It's safe in our burrow.
There's room for more."

"No!" said Scratch. "There is no room."

"We have plenty of room," said Dig.

"Thank you," said the mother wallaby.
"My lungs were filling with smoke.
I couldn't hop any farther."

The joey was glad to have a safe
place to stretch his legs.

"It's a bit crowded," complained Scratch, jostling to make space.

Now there were four animals in the burrow.

Dig spied a koala who was clinging to a branch nearby.

"Come in here with us!" called Dig. "It's safe in our home. There's still room for more."

"No!" said Scratch. "There is no room."

"We'll make room," said Dig, helping the koala inside.

"Thank you," said the koala. "My paws were burning. I couldn't get away from the fire quickly enough."

"There isn't room for anyone else, Dig," Scratch grumbled, but he squeezed over.

The five animals were safe in the burrow as smoke and flames engulfed the bush.

"Look!" said the joey. "That tiger snake is in trouble."

"Absolutely not," said Scratch. "There is no more room. Besides, tiger snakes have venom!"

The animals all looked at each other. It was indeed very squashy in the burrow now.

"But a snake doesn't take up much space," said the koala.

"Hardly any at all," agreed the mother wallaby.

"What if he bites us?" asked Scratch.

"I don't think he'll bite us," said Dig, waving the snake over.

"Thank you," said the tiger snake, sliding down the tunnel. "I thought I was going to boil."

The six animals settled in while the fire roared overhead. The mother wallaby sang songs to soothe her joey, and the other animals joined in.

All except for Scratch, who was busy keeping an eye on the tiger snake.

After many rounds of *row, row, row, your boat*,
the animals heard a pitter-patter noise on the
roof of the burrow.

The joey went to see. "It's rain!" he exclaimed.

The animals climbed out of the tunnel and cheered:
the downpour was putting out the bushfire.

But the rain didn't stop. It rained and rained until water lapped at the burrow entrance.

"We should go now," said the tiger snake.

"Thank you for your shelter," said the mother wallaby.

"Much obliged," said the koala.

"But what about us?!" cried Scratch. "We can't swim like a snake or climb like a koala. We aren't tall like a wallaby. If our home fills with water, we'll drown!"

The other animals looked at each other in dismay.

"We'll help you," said the mother wallaby. "You saved us,
so now it's our turn."

The koala and the tiger snake nodded.

The joey hopped up and down. "I want to help too!" he said.

As the rain pelted down, the animals worked together to build a barrier. They gathered rocks and piled them around the burrow entrance. They filled cracks in the wall with mud. The water was rising fast, but the animals did not give up.

Finally, the rain stopped. The barrier had held strong and kept the floodwaters out of the wombats' home.

"Thank you," said Dig. "We are so grateful for your help."

"Likewise," said the snake.

"It's the least we could do," added the koala.

"Our pleasure," said the mother wallaby. The joey climbed back into the pouch. "Good-bye, Dig!" he shouted. "Bye-bye, Scratch!"

"Aren't we clever," said Scratch, waving farewell,
"to have invited the neighbors into our home?
We might have drowned otherwise."

"Yes," agreed Dig, smiling. "We are very lucky."

AUTHOR'S NOTE:

In the devastating Australian bushfires of 2019–2020, news reports surfaced of animals finding refuge in wombat burrows. Wombats dig extensive tunnel-and-chamber burrows, so it's possible for some animals fleeing to find an empty burrow to hide in. I like to think of this as a wombat bush community service. While it isn't likely that wombats actually invited their neighbors in during the fires, their shelters have saved many lives. Yay for the wombats!

I grew up in Australia and I love to write about its unique animals and its breathtaking landscape. Because Australia is an island—the only country/continent in the world—creatures exist there that cannot be found anywhere else.

BUSHFIRES

The climate in Australia is generally hot and dry, so bushfires are common. The fires are caused by the dry conditions, lightning, or human activity. Natural oil found in the native eucalyptus trees also helps to the keep fires burning.

FLOODS

While droughts are common in Australia, often the dry conditions are broken by heavy rains. Widespread rainfall leads to a risk of floods, including flash flooding, when the waters rise very quickly. The risk of flooding is made worse when the earth is left bare of grasses and vegetation from bushfires.

CLIMATE CHANGE AND ENVIRONMENTAL DISASTERS

Environmental disasters like bushfires and floods do happen naturally. However, extreme weather like drought and heavy rains make the problem worse and climate change has made extreme weather more common. That's why it's important for us to learn how to care for our environment—all over the world—because healthy landscapes help to work against climate change.

AUSTRALIAN INDIGENOUS LAND PRACTICES

Australian Aboriginal peoples have practiced cultural burns (strategic fires) for many thousands of years to help minimize bushfires and protect wildlife. Strategic fires help to clear areas of the landscape that, if left alone, can ignite and burn out of control. In some areas of northern Australia these traditional land-management practices have been reclaimed by Indigenous rangers to help reduce bushfire risk.

GLOSSARY

WOMBATS

Wombats are short-legged and quadrupedal, meaning they walk on four feet. These **marsupials** are generally **nocturnal**, coming out at night to feed on grasses, roots, and bark. With their muscular, barrel-shaped bodies and long claws, they are champion diggers. They dig lots of tunnels with chambers for burrows.

WALLABIES

Wallabies are a smaller cousin to the kangaroo. Wallabies are marsupials and carry their young, called joeys, in a pouch. They are about half the size of a kangaroo and are bipedal, meaning they move on two feet. They are **herbivores** and eat mostly grass, as well as ferns, fruits, and leaves.

KOALAS

Koalas are tree-dwelling marsupials with large, fluffy ears. They are herbivores and eat a diet of native eucalyptus leaves. Most of their time, up to 20 hours a day, is spent sleeping because it requires a lot of energy to digest their eucalyptus diet.

TIGER SNAKES

The tiger snake is one of many **venomous** snakes found in Australia; however, it is quite shy and prefers to escape rather than bite. Tiger snakes have banded markings like tiger stripes, and they are good swimmers. They are known to live in empty animal burrows.

Marsupial
Marsupials are mammals that carry their babies in a pouch.

Nocturnal
To be nocturnal means to be active at night.

Herbivore
Herbivores feed only on plants and vegetation.

Venomous
Venomous animals, commonly snakes, can inject venom through a bite. Venom is toxic and can be harmful.